Leira Clara's Flowers

Written
by

**Doris Dearen
Settles**

Doris Settles

Illustrated
by

Dana McCall

2022

Shadelandhouse Modern Press
Lexington, Kentucky

A Shadelandhouse Modern Press book for young readers

Leira Clara's Flowers

Copyright © 2022 Doris Dearen Settles

Printed and manufactured in the United States of America
For information about permissions, please direct inquiries:
Permissions, Shadelandhouse Modern Press, LLC
P.O. Box 910913
Lexington, KY 40591
or email permissions@smpbooks.com.

Published in the United States of America by:
Shadelandhouse Modern Press, LLC, Lexington, Kentucky
smpbooks.com

First edition 2022

ISBN: 978-1-945049-27-9 (Softcover)
Library of Congress Control Number: 2022933645

ISBN: 978-1-945049-24-8 (Hardcover)
Library of Congress Control Number: 2021952826

A special thank you to May Hughes, child advisor to the publisher

Cover and interior illustrations: Dana McCall
Cover and book design: Brooke Lee

For grandniece Leira Clara
and all future generations of flower enthusiasts,
and for my grandmothers, Clara Wells Oakley and Ruth Johns Dearen,
gardeners both.

Every summer, Leira Clara went to visit her grandmother, who loved flowers. Together they grew a beautiful garden.

"Flowers make me happy," said Leira Clara to her grandmother.
"That is well and good," said Grandmother, "but flowers are
to share."

Every day, Leira Clara and her grandmother gathered a handful of the prettiest blooms and went to visit a neighbor.

Each fall, Leira Clara returned home to a yard with bushes and trees but no flowers. None of her neighbors grew flowers. Behind Mr. Thorney's shrubs and picket fence only grass grew. "How lonely," Leira Clara whispered.

Mr. Thorney yelled at children for walking on his grass. He yelled at children when their ball went in his yard. He yelled at children when their dogs barked as they passed his house. He shook his head and yelled at all the children all the time.

"Why doesn't anyone grow flowers like Grandmother?" Leira Clara asked her parents.

"We are far too busy to plant and care for a garden," huffed Leira Clara's parents.

"Too busy?" she repeated softly to herself. Leira Clara decided she was not too busy to plant and care for a garden.

She prepared the flower bed. Next, she planted flower seeds.

Leira Clara could almost hear Mr. Thorney's gravelly grumping while she worked in her garden.

Soon, Leira Clara had a garden full of flowers. She filled up every vase in the house.

Then, she remembered her grandmother's advice:

"*Flowers are to share.*"

She picked her prettiest flowers and visited a neighbor every day with a beautiful bouquet.

"What a surprise! Flowers make me happy," said Mrs. Rose.
"They make me happy, too," said Leira Clara.

"How nice!" said Mr. Daisy as Leira Clara handed him a pot of flowers. "I was feeling a little sad today. These have made me happy."

"Flowers make me happy, too," said Leira Clara, with a friendly, flowery smile. As she went about her flower-sharing, she thought of Mr. Thorney. Why was he always shaking his head and grumping?

"Why is Mr. Thorney always grumpy?" Leira Clara asked.
"I think Mr. Thorney is unhappy," replied her mother.

Leira Clara decided she would share flowers with Mr. Thorney
to make him happy.

Leira Clara went right up to Mr. Thorney's house. The big brass lion glared at her. She could hear Mr. Thorney's grumpy yelling inside the house. She wasn't sure this was a good idea after all.

"Knock"
"Knock"
"Knock"

Leira Clara turned around and left Mr. Thorney's house.

Just as she reached the sidewalk, she saw Mr. Thorney.
"I'm sharing my flowers with you," whispered Leira Clara.

"What's your name? Where did you get those? Where do you live?" yelled Mr. Thorney.

"I'm Leira Clara Bluebonnet. I live down the street, and I grew these flowers all by myself!" declared Leira Clara.

Slowly, Mr. Thorney's mouth did something strange. Was he smiling?

"I've always wanted to grow flowers," said Mr. Thorney with a quiet, sad voice.

"I'll show you!" exclaimed Leira Clara as she handed him a pot of flowers for his window.

Together they prepared the soil for Mr. Thorney's garden. Then, she shared her flower seeds for him to plant.

"Now, we wait for them to grow!" said Leira Clara.

Soon, Leira Clara and Mr. Thorney were sharing their flowers with all their friends.

Because sharing happiness is the happiest feeling of all!

Zinnias Galore!

READY! SET! GARDEN!!!

This is how Leira Clara grows her zinnias each year and you can grow them this way too.

Leira Clara is careful to give her zinnias the three most important things to grow:

- Soil
- Water
- Sun

Soil: Plant your seeds in the ground where there are no other plants, grass, or weeds. Loosen the soil with a small shovel. If you're using a pot, fill it with potting soil from the store.

Water: Like Goldilocks, zinnias like the amount of water that is just right—not too much, not too little. Leira Clara sprinkles water on her seeds after they're planted. Zinnias don't like lots of water, so no puddles! During the summer, stick your finger in the soil and if it feels wet, don't water. If it feels dry, give your zinnias a drink.

Sun: Zinnias are a full sun plant, meaning they like lots of sunlight. Plant your seeds in a spot that gets at least six hours of sunlight. They're also a summer annual, which means they'll die when it gets too cold. Plant zinnia seeds after all danger of frost in your area has passed. After she plants her seeds, Leira Clara writes ZINNIA on a Popsicle stick and marks where she planted them. And during the summer, as she's sharing and enjoying the blossoms, Leira Clara always lets some of the prettiest flowers dry out on the plant, so she can save the seeds for next year's zinnias. She cuts them off and stores them in a paper envelope with ZINNIA written on it.

Then Leira Clara is ready for next year!

Doris Settles learned to love gardening from both of her grandmothers. As an Extension Master Gardener in Kentucky, she has volunteered her time teaching others the joys of digging in the dirt. She chaired the Master Gardener Speakers Bureau for several years and speaks frequently to community groups. Her most recent book is *Leira Clara's Flowers*. Settles is also the author of *Understanding i-Kids* (Pelican Publishing 2011). Settles lives in Lexington, Kentucky, with her husband, Bill—and a quite spoiled Pomeranian—where she can be found digging in her garden and processing the fruits of her gardening labors.

Dana McCall, an eclectic self-taught artist from Winchester, Kentucky, enjoys painting in different media, including watercolor. Encouraged by her eighth-grade art teacher who saw a spark in her, McCall painted her first oil painting when she was thirteen years old. She believes that when someone has a piece of her art, they also have a piece of her heart. *Leira Clara's Flowers* is her first children's picture book. You can follow McCall's artwork on Facebook @BrushStrokesByDana.